# The Story of Prince Ivan, the Firebird, and the Gray Wolf

TRANSLATED FROM THE RUSSIAN BY THOMAS P. WHITNEY

ILLUSTRATED BY NONNY HOGROGIAN

CHARLES SCRIBNER'S SONS • NEW YORK

TRANSLATION COPYRIGHT © 1968 THOMAS P. WHITNEY / ILLUSTRATIONS COPYRIGHT © 1968 NONNY HOGROGIAN / ALL RIGHTS RESERVED / A–3–68 (RZ) / PRINTED IN THE UNITED STATES OF AMERICA / LIBRARY OF CONGRESS CATALOG CARD NUMBER 68-12521

ONCE UPON A TIME IN A CERTAIN COUNTRY THERE LIVED A KING NAMED VYSLAV ANDRONOVICH. He had three sons. The eldest was named Prince Dimitry, the next Prince Vasily, and the third Prince Ivan. This King had a park richer than any other in the world and in it grew many rare trees. The King's favorite was a tree that bore apples of gold.

There was a firebird who visited King Vyslav's park. It had golden feathers and its eyes were like oriental crystal. It would fly into the park each night, light on King Vyslav's beloved apple tree, pluck the golden apples, and fly away. King Vyslav Andronovich began to grieve over the loss of his apples, and so one day he called his sons to him and said, "My beloved children! Who of you can catch the firebird in my park? To the one who catches it alive I will give half my kingdom while I live and the other half when I die." The three princes replied in unison, "Your royal majesty, our highly esteemed sovereign and father! We will do our best to catch the firebird alive."

The first night Prince Dimitry stood guard in the park. He sat beneath the tree from which the firebird had taken the apples. But he fell asleep and did not hear the firebird come and pluck many, many of the apples. In the morning King Vyslav Andronovich sent for Prince Dimitry and asked, "Well, my beloved son, did you see the firebird?"

Prince Dimitry replied, "No, my sire and sovereign. The firebird did not come last night."

The next night Prince Vasily stood guard against the firebird. He sat beneath the apple tree till one, till two, when he also fell asleep so soundly he did not hear the firebird come and pluck the apples. In the morning King Vyslav summoned him and asked, "Well, my beloved son, did you see the firebird?"

And Prince Vasily replied, "No, my sovereign and sire. The firebird did not come last night."

The third night Prince Ivan stood guard. He sat beneath the apple tree—till one, till two, till three—and suddenly the park was lit up as if by many torches. The firebird flew in, lit on the apple tree and began to pluck the apples. Prince Ivan stole up quickly and seized it by the tail. But he could not hold on to it. All that remained in his hand was a single tailfeather.

In the morning, as soon as King Vyslav had awakened, Prince Ivan went to see him and gave him the firebird's feather. King Vyslav was delighted that his youngest son had succeeded in getting at least one feather of the firebird. The feather was so wonderful, so bright, that in a darkened room it shone like a red sun. King Vyslav placed the feather among his treasures since he wished to keep it forever. And after that the firebird no longer visited the park.

King Vyslav summoned his sons once more and said, "My beloved children! Go seek the firebird. Bring it to me alive—and to the one who brings it I will give half my kingdom while I live and the other half when I die."

Prince Dimitry and Prince Vasily were filled with spite against their younger brother, Prince Ivan, because he had succeeded in seizing a feather of the firebird. They received their father's blessing and went forth together to seek the firebird. Prince Ivan also asked his father's blessing to go in search of the bird. And even though King Vyslav did not want his last son to leave the kingdom, Prince Ivan insisted until in the end the King agreed. Prince Ivan received his father's blessing, chose a horse and rode forth, not knowing himself which way to go.

He rode and he rode—whether near or far, who can say, for tales are told swiftly but deeds are not done quickly—and came at last to green meadows and an open field. In the field stood a stone tablet inscribed with these words: *Whoever goes straight ahead will be hungry and cold. Whoever goes to the right will live, but his horse will die. Whoever goes to the left will die, but his horse will live.* After some thought, Prince Ivan decided to go to the right. He rode on for a day, two days, three, when all at once an enormous gray wolf appeared.

"Greetings, foolish Prince Ivan!" said the wolf. "Why did you come this way? You read the words on the stone tablet, that your horse would die." And having spoken, the wolf tore Prince Ivan's horse in two and ran off.

Prince Ivan wept bitterly for his horse and continued his journey on foot. He walked for a whole day and was worn out. He was just about to sit down and rest when the gray wolf caught up with him.

"I feel very sorry for you, Prince Ivan. You have tired yourself out traveling on foot. Never mind. Climb on my back, the gray wolf's back, and tell me where you want me to take you and why."

Prince Ivan explained his quest to the gray wolf, and the wolf sped off with the Prince on his back. After a time—it was night, as it happened—the wolf came to a stone wall which was not very high. He stopped and said, "Now, Prince Ivan, jump off my back, off the gray wolf's back, and climb over that stone wall. Behind the wall is a park, and in the park the firebird sits in a golden cage. Take the firebird but do not touch the golden cage, for otherwise you will be caught on the spot."

Prince Ivan climbed over the stone wall into the park, saw the firebird in the golden cage and immediately took a fancy to it. He removed the bird and started back, but then he thought to himself, "Why did I take the firebird without its cage? How will I carry it?" He returned to the cage, but just as he took hold of it there was a rumbling and clanging throughout the park. The guards woke up, rushed into the park and caught Prince Ivan with the firebird. They took him to their King, who was called Dolmat. King Dolmat was very angry with Prince Ivan and raged at him in a loud and wrathful voice, "You should be ashamed to steal, foolish youth! What country do you come from? Who is your father? And what is your name?"

Prince Ivan replied, "I am the son of King Vyslav Andronovich and my name is Prince Ivan. Your firebird used to come to our park every night and steal golden apples from my father's favorite tree. That is why my father sent me to find the firebird and bring it back to him."

"Foolish youth, Prince Ivan!" King Dolmat declared. "Is it proper to do as you have done? Had you come to me, I would have given you the firebird as a gift. Now what have you gained? For I must proclaim throughout all kingdoms how dishonorably you have acted in my country. But listen to me, Prince Ivan! If you fulfill my wish and journey through thirty lands and nine and in the fortieth get for me King Afron's steed with the golden mane, I will grant you a pardon and give you the firebird with honor."

Prince Ivan grew very sad. He returned to the gray wolf and told him all that King Dolmat had said.

"You foolish youth, Prince Ivan," the gray wolf declared. "Why didn't you heed what I told you? Why did you touch the golden cage?"

"I know what I did was wrong. Forgive me, gray wolf," said Prince Ivan.

"Very well," said the gray wolf. "Climb on my back, the gray wolf's back, and I will take you where you need to go."

Prince Ivan climbed on the gray wolf's back and the wolf ran as swiftly as an arrow—near or far, who can say?—and in the end, at night, he came to the kingdom of King Afron. On approaching the royal white-stone stables, the gray wolf said to Prince Ivan, "Go into the stables, Prince Ivan, and bring out the steed with the golden mane. Just one thing: on the wall hangs a golden bridle. Do not take it, for it will bring you misfortune."

Prince Ivan went into the stables, took hold of the horse and was about to leave when he saw the golden bridle hanging on the wall. He liked it so much that he lifted it off its nail. Immediately there was a clanging and clatter throughout the stables. The stable guards rushed in, caught Prince Ivan and brought him to King Afron.

"Foolish youth," said the King. "What country do you come from? Who is your father? And what is your name?"

Prince Ivan replied, "I am the son of King Vyslav Andronovich and my name is Prince Ivan."

"Foolish Prince Ivan," King Afron said to him. "Is this the deed of an honest nobleman? Had you asked me, I would have given you the steed with the golden mane as a gift. Now what have you gained? For I must proclaim throughout all kingdoms how dishonorably you have acted in my country. Nonetheless, listen to me, Prince Ivan! If you fulfill my wish and journey through thirty lands and nine and in the fortieth get for me Princess Elena the Beautiful, whom I love with all my heart and soul but whom I cannot win, I will grant you a pardon and will give you, in good faith, the steed with the golden mane and the golden bridle. If you do not fulfill my wish I will proclaim in all the kingdoms that you are dishonest and a thief."

Prince Ivan left the palace, weeping bitterly. He returned to the gray wolf and told him everything that had happened.

"You foolish youth, Prince Ivan," declared the gray wolf. "Why did you not heed my words? Why did you take the golden bridle?"

"I know I was wrong. Forgive me, gray wolf," said Prince Ivan.

"Very well," declared the gray wolf, "Climb on my back, the gray wolf's back, and I will take you where you need to go."

Prince Ivan got on the gray wolf's back and the wolf ran as swiftly as an arrow and at last arrived in the country of Princess Elena the Beautiful. The wolf stopped at a lovely park surrounded by a golden fence and said to Prince Ivan, "Climb down off my back, the gray wolf's back, and return along this road. Wait for me in that open field by the green oak."

Prince Ivan did as he was told. The gray wolf sat near the golden fence and waited for Princess Elena the Beautiful to take a walk in the park. In the evening when the sun began to sink far to the west, Princess Elena came out to the park, attended by her maids and the noble ladies of the court. When she reached the place where the gray wolf sat, he leaped over the fence into the park, seized the Princess and ran off with her as fast as he could. He brought her to the open field beneath the green oak where Prince Ivan was waiting and said, "Prince Ivan, jump quickly on my back, the gray wolf's back."

Prince Ivan mounted the gray wolf and the wolf dashed off carrying them both to the country of King Afron. The maids and all the ladies of the court hurried to the palace to send horsemen in pursuit of the Princess. But no matter how fast they rode, they could not catch up with the gray wolf and finally were forced to turn back.

As soon as Prince Ivan had seated himself on the gray wolf together with Princess Elena the Beautiful, he fell in love with her and she with him. And as the gray wolf neared the country of King Afron, the Prince became very sad and began to weep. The gray wolf asked him why he was weeping and Prince Ivan replied, "My friend, gray wolf, how can I not weep and be sad? I have fallen in love with Princess Elena and now I must give her away to King Afron in exchange for the steed with the golden mane. If I do not deliver her to King Afron, he will proclaim my dishonor to all the kingdoms."

"I have served you well," said the gray wolf. "And I will help you now. Listen to me, Prince Ivan. I am going to transform myself into Princess Elena the Beautiful, and when I do you are to take me to King Afron. In return he will give you the steed with the golden mane because he will mistake me for the real Princess. Mount the steed with the golden mane and ride off. When you are far away, on the fourth day, I will ask permission of King Afron to take a walk in the meadow. Once I am out in the meadow with the maids and the ladies of the court, you will remember me and I will be with you again in an instant."

The gray wolf finished speaking, stamped on the ground and became the Princess Elena. Prince Ivan instructed the real Princess Elena to wait for him outside the city and took the false princess, the gray wolf, to the palace of King Afron. King Afron was overjoyed to receive the treasure he had so long desired. He gave the steed with the golden mane to Prince Ivan, who mounted it and rode out of the city to the real Princess Elena the Beautiful. He seated her beside him and they continued on in the direction of King Dolmat's country.

The gray wolf lived with King Afron for one day, two and three, as Princess Elena the Beautiful, and on the fourth day went to King Afron to ask permission to go for a walk in the meadow to help relieve her homesickness. King Afron replied, "My beautiful Princess Elena! I will do anything to please you," and he ordered the maids and the ladies of the court to accompany the Princess to the meadow.

Meanwhile Prince Ivan was riding along with Princess Elena the Beautiful and talking with her, not thinking of the gray wolf. But on the fourth day he suddenly remembered. "Oh, where is my gray wolf?" he said. And from out of nowhere the gray wolf stood before him.

"Climb on my back, the gray wolf's back, Prince Ivan, and let the beautiful Princess ride on the horse with the golden mane."

Prince Ivan mounted the gray wolf and they continued on their way until they arrived at the land of King Dolmat. Whether they rode for a long time or a short time, who can say? But at last they stopped about three miles from the city. Here Prince Ivan said to the gray wolf, "My kind friend, gray wolf! You have fulfilled all my wishes. Grant me one last wish. I don't want to part with the steed with the golden mane. Would you transform yourself into the steed with the golden mane so that I can keep the real one?"

The gray wolf immediately stamped on the ground and became the steed with the golden mane. Prince Ivan left Princess Elena the Beautiful in a green meadow with the real steed with the golden mane, mounted the false steed, the gray wolf, and rode to the palace of King Dolmat.

No sooner had he arrived than King Dolmat saw Prince Ivan riding the steed with the golden mane and came out of his palace into the broad courtyard to meet him. He embraced him warmly, took him by the right hand and led him into his white-stone palace. King Dolmat ordered a feast prepared to celebrate the joyous occasion. The guests sat down at oaken tables covered with damask tablecloths. They drank, ate, amused themselves and made merry for exactly two days, and on the third day King Dolmat presented Prince Ivan with the firebird and the golden cage.

Prince Ivan took the firebird and returned outside the city to Princess Elena the Beautiful. Both mounted the real steed with the golden mane and rode off toward Prince Ivan's homeland.

On the next day King Dolmat decided to take a ride in the country on his steed with the golden mane. But the false steed threw King Dolmat, turned himself back into the gray wolf and ran off to catch up with Prince Ivan.

"Prince Ivan," he said, "climb on my back, the gray wolf's back, and let Princess Elena the Beautiful ride on the steed with the golden mane."

Prince Ivan mounted the gray wolf and they continued on together. As soon as the gray wolf had brought Prince Ivan back to the place where he had torn apart the Prince's horse, he stopped and said, "Well, Prince Ivan, I have served you faithfully and well, and I have brought you back to where I tore your horse in two. Climb off my back, the gray wolf's back. Now you have the steed with the golden mane, and I am your servant no longer."

The gray wolf, after saying these words, ran off. Prince Ivan wept bitterly for the gray wolf and went on his way with Princess Elena the Beautiful.

They both rode on the horse with the golden mane—for a long time or a short time, who can say?—until they came within a dozen miles of Prince Ivan's homeland. There they stopped to rest. They dismounted, and Prince Ivan tied the steed with the golden mane to a tree and placed the cage with the firebird at his side. Lying next to each other on the soft grass beneath the tree, they fell fast asleep.

At that moment, Prince Ivan's brothers, Prince Dimitry and Prince Vasily, who had traveled through many countries without finding the firebird, were returning home empty-handed. They came upon their sleeping brother and Princess Elena the Beautiful. Seeing the steed with the golden mane and the firebird in its golden cage, and wanting these treasures for themselves, they decided to kill their brother, Prince Ivan. Prince Dimitry drew his sword from its scabbard and ran Prince Ivan through.

Then he awakened the beautiful Princess and asked, "Beautiful maiden! What country do you come from? Who is your father? And what is your name?"

Princess Elena, seeing Prince Ivan dead, became frightened and began to cry bitterly. "I am Princess Elena the Beautiful, and I was won by Prince Ivan, whom you have foully murdered. Had you gone out to fight him openly in the field and won victory over him alive, you might have been called brave warriors. But you killed him in his sleep. What glory have you won by such a deed? A sleeping man is as helpless as a dead man."

Prince Dimitry pointed his sword at the heart of Princess Elena and said, "Listen to me. We will take you to our father, King Vyslav Andronovich, and you must tell him that we won you and the firebird and the steed with the golden mane. If you do not promise to do as we say, I will kill you right away!"

Princess Elena the Beautiful was so terrified, she swore by all that is holy that she would repeat what she had been told to say. Then Prince Dimitry and Prince Vasily cast lots to see who would get the beautiful Princess and who the steed with the golden mane. The Princess fell to Prince Vasily and the steed with the golden mane to Prince Dimitry.

Prince Ivan had been lying on that spot for thirty days when the gray wolf came upon his body and recognized him. The gray wolf wanted to help Prince Ivan, to bring him back to life, but he didn't know how. Just then, the gray wolf saw a crow and two of its young flying over the body, preparing to land and devour the flesh of Prince Ivan. The gray wolf hid behind a bush, and as soon as the young crows lit on Prince Ivan, the gray wolf jumped out from behind the bush, grabbed one young crow and started to tear it in two. At this point the old crow landed at a safe distance from the gray wolf and called, "My greetings, gray wolf. Do not harm my child. After all, he has done you no harm."

And the gray wolf replied, "Listen to me, oh crow, you son of a crow. I will not harm your offspring if you fulfill my wish. Fly off through thirty lands and nine and in the fortieth find and bring to me both water dead and water living."

And the crow, the son of a crow, said, "I will fulfill your wish—if you do not harm my son." The crow uttered these words and flew away. On the third day the crow returned with two vials of water, one filled with water living and the other with water dead. The gray wolf took the vials. Then he tore the young crow in two and sprayed him with water dead and the crow grew together again. He sprinkled him with water living and the crow fluttered and flew away. Now the gray wolf sprinkled Prince Ivan with the water dead and his wounded body became whole. He sprinkled him with water living and Prince Ivan rose and said, "How is it that I slept so long?"

To which the gray wolf replied, "You would have slept for eternity, Prince Ivan, had it not been for me. Your own brothers murdered you and took away Princess Elena the Beautiful, the steed with the golden mane and the firebird. You must hurry home as fast as you can. Your brother, Prince Vasily, is to marry Princess Elena the Beautiful today. Climb on my back, the gray wolf's back, and I will carry you there."

Prince Ivan mounted the gray wolf, who sped with him to the kingdom of King

Vyslav Andronovich. Whether it took them a long time or a short time, who can say?

But after a while they arrived at the city gates.

Prince Ivan dismounted and entered the city. Arriving at the palace he found his brother, Prince Vasily, with Princess Elena the Beautiful at a celebration feast before their wedding. Princess Elena saw Prince Ivan and immediately got up from the table, ran to him, and cried, "This is my beloved bridegroom, Prince Ivan, and not that evildoer who sits there at the table!"

King Vyslav Andronovich rose from his place to question Princess Elena the Beautiful, and the Princess told him all that had happened. King Vyslav had Prince Dimitry and Prince Vasily imprisoned in a dungeon. Prince Ivan married Princess Elena the Beautiful and they lived so happily together that neither could be without the other for even a single moment.